A whistle from the hill.

Chapter 1.

" There are many unsung heroes of the second world war and I'm going to get them

 recognised". Jim dictated into his voice recorder.

He placed it down onto his desk and leaned back into his chair.

For as long as he could remember, he was deeply into history.

To him there was nothing better. So, he studied hard at school, college and university and gained the expertise to become a teacher of history.

Within a year of qualifying, he entered his job in the local primary school.

It wasn't his ideal placement, but he knew that within a few years, he may be able to move up a level, to secondary schools. Within ten years, he had

continued to study, as well as teach and had progressed to a professor of history at the university.

On his journey of education, he had met people from all walks of life assist him gaining his expertise.

His particular field of history was world war two.

If anyone wanted to know anything about the subject, he was the man to go too.

He placed his hands up behind his head and stared at the paperwork in the desk.

Amongst the papers of essays from pupils and books that he was studying through, was an airline ticket.

This was his summer holiday.

Jim always planned his summer break a year ahead of itself. he would meticulously plan everything.

The previous year, he visited Dieppe in northern France and roamed the town, taking the history and studying the war sights.

He started by going to the eawy forest, home of the v1 bomber launch sights.

The end of his trip was in Dieppe itself, where he visited ' Le memorial du 19 aout 1942 '.

Sat laid back in his chair, he could picture the sights and the friends he had made on his trip.

He could visualise the picture that sat on his bookshelf in his mind.

Four friends that he met and himself, standing outside the museum.

Jim was a little worried, when he asked a teenage boy if he could take the photo.

He was concerned that he may kiss goodbye to a thousand pounds worth of camera.

but It turned out, that the lad was in fact the nephew of the museum's curator.

Within minutes, the picture was taken, and the lad was on his way off down the road.

This year, his adventure would take him to Zeus's birthplace, Crete.

All the details had been finalised.

Lodgings and all transport were arranged and paid for.

Jim would land and stay at Heraklion for two days, then west to Maleme for two more days and would slowly work his way south, to the coastal town of Sfakia.

So, for the next two weeks, he would go over maps, old and new, so he could plan all the locations he would try to visit.

Jim knew some of the history of Crete, particularly during the war in 1941 when the German Fallschirmjager dropped onto the island and fought long and hard to take it from allied hands.

He studied the battle for one of his term papers and received an a star for his work.

Two weeks passed quickly.

The students had left for summer break and all the paperwork was finished and put to one side ready for collection.

Jim had his bag packed and it was standing by the door waiting for the taxi to arrive.

soon he would be at the airport and boarding the plane.

Taking his phone from his pocket, he unlocks the screen and begins scrolling through his contacts.

He stops when he gets to the name Costantinos and presses the call button.

It rings twice then goes quiet.

" Hi Costa " Jim calls out.

There continues to be a pause, then quietly " ah hello Jim, how are you? "

Jim smiles, " I'm good thanks, just checking in before I leave for the airport".

He had hardly finished speaking when costa quickly replied " all is good jim,

I will be at the airport for you at 2 in the afternoon ".

" perfect " jim replied, " see you then, by for now ". and he hung up the phone.

No sooner had he put his phone back in his pocket, than he heard the taxi pull up outside and toot his horn.

Jim silently said goodbye to his home, opened the front door and stepped outside.

Every other step, he would turn his head and look at his house. By the time he got to the taxi, he had looked back ten times. the last look he wished the house farewell and stepped into the car.

Jim made himself comfortable and placed his seatbelt around him and clicked it in place.

" where to? " the driver called.

" the airport please " Jim replied.

Jim knew this driver, George had taken him to the university a few times, when his car was out of action.

He opened his bag and took out one of his books. a tour guide to Crete.

" hey George, where in Greece are you from? " Jim asked.

" me, I'm from kerkyra - Corfu. you heading to Greece? " George replied.

" yes, I'm heading to Crete " he replied.

" a lovely island, I have family there, lots of history ".

Jim smiled and George saw this in the rear-view mirror.

" I take it you are going on one of your history trips again?" George asked.

" yes, the battle of Crete this time ".

George let out a faint sniff. " please make sure you visit the graves of our forefathers and friends in Souda and Anogia ".

Part of one of Jims papers was about the destruction of the town of Anogia.

He remembered the loss of life and the total destruction of the village by the Germans after German general Kriepe was taken prisoner. They ordered all men withing the village up to one kilometre away, would be rounded up and executed.

some had escaped to the hills and some went to nearby villages, in an attempt to evade capture. thirty-seven people lost their lives.

Rethinking about this saddened Jim, " I will " he replied. "I know quite a bit

about what happened there".

As George drove the taxi into the drop off point, he looked back at Jim.

" my aunt still lives there in Anogia, by the hotel Psiloritis, I can call

her, she can talk to you about what happened". jim was going to try to find an excuse not to visit Georges aunt and was just about to play it down, but realised that, she would be able to give him a first-hand statement of what happened.

Jim handed George ten pounds for the journey and stepped out of the car.

" I will " Jim replied.

As he walked round to the back of the cab, George walked up, placed the ten pounds back in Jims hand " there's no need to pay , you are doing me a great deed " Jim reluctantly accepted and placed the money back into his wallet.

George agreed to contact his aunt and they exchanged numbers.

They wished each other well and Jim walked into the terminal.

Jim was never too keen on airports, ' too much waiting around ' he thought, but it was still the quickest way to get there.

He checked in and went and sat in the departure lounge with a coffee, there he waited for another two hours before they were called onto the plane.

The flight would last four hours, Jim compensated this by having plenty of reading material and had downloaded a few documentaries of interest onto his iPad.

However, once the aircraft reached its cruising altitude, Jim had fallen asleep.

He didn't wake until the captain called for passengers to put on their seatbelts and that they were preparing for landing.

On arrival, the cabin crew opened the doors. Jim could feel the heat flood through the plane. Jim turned to a little boy sitting next to him.

" phew, it's going to be hot " and giggled. The boy laughed in reply before he was distracted by his parents wanting to get off as quickly as possible.

He wasn't too bothered how quick he got off the plane. So, he just sat there and waited for most of the passengers to evacuate. Jim slowly got out of his seat and made his way to the front of the plane. There were still a few passengers

remaining on board, but by now it wasn't so hectic. he stopped when he got to the door. He took a deep breath, he turned to the stewardess, smiled " there's always that holiday smell when you get off " and stepped off onto the aircraft steps.

Most airconditioned places were the same, but Jim couldn't resist the quip.

With him only having his large hold all, he was able to get through the airport quickly. he arrived at the taxi rank and waited for his contact to arrive.

He only waited ten minutes and Costa; his contact pulled in.

Costa was a thin man, with a deep black goatee and well dressed.

h greeted Jim with a bear hug type grip.

They became friends a few years prior after they met at a lecture held at the university. When costa announced he was returning to Crete, Jim jumped at the

chance to keep in touch.

As a result, they became solid friends and it was costa that persuaded jim to

come to Crete instead of his previous plan of the Normandy beaches.

" hello Costa, been a while " jim said receiving Costas hug.

" Hey Jim, good to see you " Costa replied.

He took Jims bag and placed it in the boot. they sat down in the front of the car.

Costa was a proud Greek and loved his country. hanging from the rear-view mirror was a small cloth Greek flag and dangling loosely underneath was a sea blue cross and tassel of the same colours as the national flag.

Under that propped up on the dashboard was a picture of his family.

His mother and father proudly placed in the middle, surrounded by sons, daughters,

grandsons and granddaughters.

Jim point to the photo, " how is the family? ".

Costa sighed, " Father isn't too well Jim, he has stayed in bed for the last week.

He says he has no energy ".

Costas father was a worker, he worked extremely hard from a very young age, he was six when the Germans invaded the island in

1941 and had to work their olive farms after his father decided to leave and fight for the resistance. He hadn't really stopped. The family had told him to ease off and now his body was starting to react.

Jim grinned " maybe the rest is what he needs, he has never stopped has he?".

" No, he hasn't and now he has no choice but to stop, we are there for him though ".

The conversation was short, Jim had booked a hotel close to the airport and not too far from Costas home.

The hotel Sofia was quite a large hotel, quaintly decorated and flying their flag honourably, everywhere Jim looked.

Costa pulled up to the reception and jim opened his door.

" will you come to my home for dinner later Jim " Costa asks.

Jim picked up his bag " I would love to Costa. I'm going to check in and freshen up first "

" of course, I will call you in two hours " Costa replied.

" excellent, speak to you soon " and jim walked into the building.

Within forty minutes, he had unpacked the holdall, had his shower and had poured

 himself an ice-cold water from the fridge. Now he was sitting on his balcony, with his drink and staring out at the landscape laid before him and listening to his surroundings. The sounds of mopeds buzzing back and forth down the streets,

people meeting and chatting. This amused Jim, he found it amusing. He had asked himself many times ' why do the Greeks sound like they are arguing ', he felt the

Language was aggressive, even though they could be talking about bread rolls.

His phone rings, its Costa.

" Hello Jim, is six o'clock ok for me to come for you? ".

" of course, that's fine, I will be waiting for you ".

Costa says something in Greek away from the phone and the returns to speaking with Jim.

" ok, see you later, my family cannot wait to see you "

and the phone hung up.

Jim looked at his watch, he had an hour, plenty of time to do some research.

He walked into the room and picked up a couple of small books from off the bedside table and sat back out on the balcony.

Jim looked at the first book, it was about Anogia. Jim would read books a few times, in case he missed anything the previous time.

As this was going to be his first visit, he decided that he would flip through that one first.

Jims time on the balcony flew by and didn't seem like long at all when his phone buzzed a reminder.

He placed the books back on the bedside table and made his way down to the hotel reception to wait for Costa.

Their meal was an honest one. Costas wife, mother and grandmother had been kept busy all day, putting the food together. Upon jim and Costas arrival, the family

all came out to greet them.

Jim felt embarrassed, he didn't feel comfortable being welcomed like he was royalty.

They ushered him inside and sat him down at the table. The ladies had produced an amazing spread of food.

The food was going to take a while to eat, but with the good company Jim was with, it would prove to be a great evening.

Most of the conversations were about life in general, what everyone did for work and leisure and families. It was a few hours into the evening when they were all sitting outside in the garden with drinks, when Costas grandmother sat beside Jim. She turned to face him and smiled. Then proceeded to talk to him in Greek.

Costa, who was sitting at the end of the group came over and began to translate.

" she wants to know what you are hoping to find here "

Jim laughed " I'm glad you're here, I think I'm going to need you ".

They both laughed.

" I'm here for knowledge " he replied.

Costa then repeated Jims words to his grandmother, as he did, she started nodding.

" I'm here to learn about what happened here when the Germans invaded during the war, where did the people go when they attacked and hear some stories about the resistance ".

Suddenly, Grandmothers face went from the look of interested, to one of sadness.

She mumbled something to Costa, turned and look at Jim.

Jim knew something upset her.

" Have i said something wrong?" jim asked.

Costas mother Anna stepped in, she had seen the conversation start and felt intrigued by the conversation. She moved her chair closer.

" She wants to know if you are going to Anogia?".

" is there something wrong with me going there?" he replied.

While Jim and Anna were talking Costas, grandmother was still talking with Costa.

Finally, after a few minutes, Costa turned towards Jim and Anna.

" my grandmother has asked that you stay off the hills that look over the town "

" what's with the hills " Jim replied.

Costas father jumped into the conversation.

" it will play with your mind jim, best you don't go there ".

Costa took hold of his grandmothers' hands.

" MY grandmother and family came from Anogia, they all left when the Germans attacked ".

Jim was feeling tired up to this point, now he was wide awake and intrigued by what Costas grandmother was now saying.

" this was the town that was raised to the ground?". he asked.

Costa had stopped speaking with his grandmother.

" yes jim, the Germans entered the town after one of their high-ranking officers was kidnapped by the resistance. anyone that was with the resistance left for the hills, the rest were forced out of the town before it was completely destroyed".

Jim sat silently, stunned by the information that was coming forward from Costas family.

Costas grandmother started talking again and Anna translated almost instantly.

Jim had now changed his seating position and almost looked like the statue ' the thinker '.

" she is saying please don't go into the hills. the town has been rebuilt, but the hills are still haunted by the past "

Jim raised an eyebrow.

"What do you mean, haunted by the past?" Jim asked.

"There are many strange things that have happened in the hills, since the town was destroyed. Most of the people don't talk about it".

"is it all to do with what happened during the war?".

Anna looked sheepishly at Jim.

"it was because of the war that the people do not go into the hills, bad things happen there".

Now it was Costas turn to say something "I really don't think it's a good idea that you go into the hills, my grandmother says not too, then you need to take her advice. I have driven past many times and the place creeps me out. I heard as a boy never to go there, we heard stories of a man that went into the hills and two days later he returned completely scared out of his mind. He apparently kept talking about hearing strange noises and decided to investigate, no-one knows what he found, only that it made him mad".

Jim knew most of the history about the battle of Crete but had never heard anything like what he was hearing now.

He did not look into the paranormal, but what Costas family were talking about now, fell into that category.

Intrigue set in again and this now made Jim more determined to find out what had happened.

He had subconsciously decided that he would have to investigate the town of Anogia, particularly the hills.

The conversation turned and the subject matter changed. After an hour, it was time to head back to the hotel, as it was getting late and Jim wanted to get some more research into Anogia done before the morning.

Once in his hotel room, he sat on his bed and started to read through the small books of notes that he had made before he left home.

Within minutes, he was fast asleep. Not realising that the hills of Anogia had already set into his mind. In his dreams he was picturing the hills, but they looked different and there were strange noises coming from them.

There were no noises from the wildlife, but he could hear distant gunfire and the occasional explosion.

Suddenly everything went black, there was a void, a dark coldness and the air was stale and musty. The only sound he could now hear, was a faint whistling.

There was a flash of light that momentarily dazed him, when his vision returned, he was standing on the largest of the hills overlooking the town.

As he was looking into the town, he hadn't realised that someone was walking up behind him.

"Achtung halt!".

Jim loses his footing and falls backwards over the edge of the steep embankment and starts to fall.

As he drops towards the ground, the nightmare starts to fade and the last thing he sees before he wakes, is the amused look on a German soldier's face.

He wakes suddenly, soaked with sweat.

Jim freshened himself up, got dressed and went downstairs for breakfast.

For an hour, he sat at the table, going through his mind at what had happened in his dream.

It scared him. Why was he dreaming of Anogia, the hills and the German soldier?

Did this man push him off the cliff?

The waiter came over with some coffee, he could see Jim was upset about something.

"are you ok sir?" he asked.

Jim looked up.

"yes, I'm fine thank you, just didn't sleep too well last night".

The waiter was very friendly and had previously asked jim about his purpose for visiting Crete.

He looked at Jim with concerned eyes. "Where are you going too today?" he asked.

"I'm heading into Anogia today".

"be careful there, sir, keep to the town and stay away from the eastern hills".

Jim rolled his eyes "why does everyone keep telling me to stay away from the hills? What is so special about them?".

Jim had not realised that he had risen his voice and several people had turned their heads to check out the commotion.

The waiter stepped back "there is bad energy there and bad things happen in those hills" and with that he turned and walked back into the kitchen.

Jim was intending on going straight out, after he had eaten his breakfast.

So, he had brought his rucksack into the restaurant with him.

When sat down, he neatly tucked it underneath, so as to be in no-one's way.

Now he was rifling through the bag, trying to find one of his notebooks. The one he was after had nestled its way to the bottom, making him reach further and further inside. His hand clasped around it, he withdrew it from the bag and placed it on the table.

He then started to flick through the pages, he stopped at a section of the notebook he had titled places to visit for information.

While sipping his coffee, he ticked the places he would go to first to try and get as much information as possible.

He was unaware of someone watching him from the kitchen.

He picked up his bag from under the table and started to walk out of the restaurant. As he did, his watcher slowly walked out of the kitchen and began to follow him out of the restaurant, through the reception and out onto the street.

Jim took a deep breath and received a cacophony of smells into his nostrils.

The heat combined with various smells of the restaurants along the street, sent images into his mind. He could picture the things he was smelling, which made him smile.

He studied his notebook briefly, took his phone out of his pocket and opened the map application.

He entered the first address that he'd placed in his notebook and waited.

A few minutes passed and his phone sprung into life. Jim looked at the screen, looked to his left and stepped onto the pavement and began to walk along the street.

Jim was totally unaware of the frail old man following behind.

Finally, he arrived at his chosen location, a local government centre for records.

He was determined find some more information on the town and the disaster that struck it.

Before he could walk up the steps to the main doors, there was a tap on his shoulder.

He turned and came face to café with the man that had followed him from the hotel.

"can I help you?" Jim asked.

"sorry, yes. Nikos the waiter from the hotel told me why you are here in Crete".

Jim was a little confused and angry that his business was being talked about with others, then realised that if he didn't want people to know, then he shouldn't have said anything in the first place.

He smiled and held out his hand.

The old man knew what he was attempting to do and shook it rigorously.

"I can help you more than this office can, there will be no records here. There are non-anywhere". He replied.

"come with me and I will explain" and he beckoned Jim away from the building.

After a few minutes walking, they arrived at a small taverna. He signalled for Jim to sit down and he walked up to the bar.

Moments later, he returned with two coffees and with shaking hands, placed them onto the table and sat down opposite Jim.

Chapter 2

The day was hot jim was not really interested in coffee, but he would except the drink anyway. They sat in silence for a few minutes. The old man coughed and was the first to break the silence.

"You must excuse my approach" he started

"I worked in the hotel Nikos the waiter told me why you were here in Crete and I feel I need to share with you the reason why we do not go into the hills"

Jim suddenly felt glad that he had not gone into the offices and taken a walk with the old man instead.

"I was 12 when the Germans arrived my father was from the resistance and lived in Anogia"

He took a sip of coffee and continued

"they had kidnapped a field marshal or some high-ranking officer the Germans were not happy, and they entered the town. We knew they were coming so all the men and boys were helped in their plight left the town and headed into the hills behind the monastery".

Jim finished his coffee straight away he knew all this information and was not being told anything he didn't already know.

"this I already know my friend" he replied

"yes, but what you don't know all of is what happened after"

Jim shuffled his chair closer to the table

"carry on then I'm intrigued" and he clasped his hands together

"all the women and children were removed from the town as you probably know already, they then destroyed it then continued to search for the rest of us that had hidden. They caught and executed dozens, but the rest of us stayed hidden until the area was clear of Germans. It was not until we caught up with our families that we found out what the Germans did to those they had caught. In those tales there was one that scared us, and this is what stops us from going there to this day."

"scared you?" Jim asked

"yes, many others and I will not go back there, and we make it our responsibility to warn people away from the area"

"what if I don't listen to your advice" jim was now starting to get annoyed with him.

"be it on you if you do not take my advice. Let me explain why first we were told that a group of friends and our family that had gone to the area of the hills had been followed by the Germans. They found the sillies and hid inside them"

Jim had not got a clue as to what sillies were and did not want to sound uneducated and acknowledged what he was saying anyway.

Within a few minutes, it was all revealed and Jim was shocked.

The man continued his story.

"The remaining men had found the Scillies to hide in, only the pursuing Germans could see where they were going. They surrounded the area and waited for them to come out.

After many warnings, none of them would come out, so the Germans set explosives around the entrances and blew them up".

"oh my god, that's bad "Jim replied in shock.

"it continues, since then, anyone that has journeyed into the hills has heard things. Things they cannot explain. Voices. but most of all whistling".

"whistling?"

"Yes, from the hills themselves. I went there a few years after the war had ended with some of my friends, we all heard the whistles.

A few of us heard voices as well. We tried to locate the sounds, but nothing. We looked in the area of the scillies, nothing.

The entrance had been completely covered".

Jim was getting amused by the ghost story that the old man was telling him, his amusement was soon going to change to one of shock.

"We then went back to the town, which was slowly coming back to life and told people what had happened. we were scolded for going there. My friends mother told us, that only one person managed to escape, only to get taken back by the soldier's. They wanted to know how he escaped. He wouldn't tell them, so an officer took him to the cliff edge and gave him one last chance. He still would not tell them, so he was pushed off the cliff to his death".

Jim sat back in his chair in terror and sweat started pouring from his head.

'This cant be from my dream, surely' he thought.

"You are uncomfortable with this information?" the man asked.

"I'm fine "Jim replied "carry on".

The man just sat back in his chair, finished his coffee and sat staring directly at Jim.

Jim could clearly see tears in his eyes.

"My father was one of those men that went into those caves. I wanted to go and get his body back for my mother. We never went back.

We have tried to warn people of what goes on in those hills, a few have ignored them and have come back terrified. Now you are here. I can only repeat those warnings. Visit the monastery, pay your respects at the memorial there, if you value your sanity, you will not go any further".

With that, he stood up, shook Jims hand and walked off down the road towards the hotel.

Jim walked up to the bar. He wanted to study his notes further as he was close to the monastery. He would stay there, have another drink and go through them.

He waited a few minutes and the barman appeared from out of the back, balancing a tray in his hands.

"be one moment sir" he called out, as he skipped between the tables and chairs to a group of tourists.

He returned behind the bar and towards Jim.

"what would you like please?" He asked.

"I will have the same as before" Jim replied.

"What did you have?"

"Whatever the old man ordered for us earlier"

"What old man? You came alone. You sat down there for the last twenty minutes and never ordered anything, you just sat there looking towards the hills".

Jim turned to look where he was sitting. There were no cups on the table and the barman hadn't collected them.

A shiver rippled down Jims spine. For the sake of Jims sanity, He didn't say anything else apart from what he wanted to drink.

"Just an iced latte please "he replied and walked back to the table and took his seat.

A few moments passed and the barman returned with the coffee, placed it on the table in front of Jim.

"Are you touring?" he asked.

"educational visit" Jim replied.

The barman tutted and walked back behind the bar.

Jim rifled through his bag, picked out a few of the notebooks and began to flick through the pages. He stopped when he came across a page that described the monastery.

The monument was in his notes, but he didn't realise that it had any relevance to what happened in the hills. He thought it was just a general memorial to all of those that had died.

He jumped when suddenly his phone buzzed in his pocket. he withdrew it and looked at the screen.

It was George the taxi driver.

He pressed the screen to accept the call and held the phone to his ear.

"Hi George, how are you?" Jim asks.

The reply was fast "Hi Jim. My auntie will not be able to meet you. She has gone to see family in Corfu and will not be back for at least a month. I'm sorry my friend".

Jim was not too sure whether to be happy or not. It seemed to him, that he was doing just fine.

"George, that's fine. Don't worry about it. I will go and pay my respects as you asked". He felt a little sad for George, as he had given him a free ride to the airport. He would make up for it when he returned to the UK.

"I will see you when I return George"

"Ok Jim, see you soon "and hung up the phone.

He picked up his latte, sat back in the chair and admired the scenery in the sun. His next plan would be to go to the monastery. If he were going to find out any more information, it would be there.

He checked his maps application to see how far the monastery was from his current location.

Fortunately, it was only a short ten-minute walk away.

He sat for a while rummaging through his notes.

All the information for that area neatly fitted on to four pages. Before he left the UK, it looked like the main point of interest would be hill 107 at Malame.

This now changed and he started to get the feeling that he would be spending all of his time at Anogia.

He finished his drink, slung his rucksack over his shoulder and walked to the bathroom.

On his way back out, he waved goodbye to the barman and walked out into the street. He could see the monastery in front of him, a little way down the road. A foreboding looking building that even from a distance appeared to bare the scares of what happened many years before. Parts of the walls were still missing.

As he walked, he felt like he was being watched, like a cowboy in the westerns walking to a duel and the residents would be peering from behind net curtains or doors.

He felt uneasy, the whole road was devoid of people and cars.

On the previous road, there were plenty.

This was a main road and Jim was curious as to the change.

As Jim approached the outskirts of the town, the monastery became much clearer. Not only could he see shell marks on the unkept walls, but now he could make out the small individual bullet holes. He thought, how strange it was that after all this time, that no one had cared to fix it.

He could make out the sound of someone giggling, turned and saw two old men sitting on a porch in a run-down building, which Jim could only put down to being one of their homes.

He heard one of them muttering something to the other. Not knowing any Greek, he was none the wiser as to what they were saying.

When he looked again, they were both shaking their heads. This angered him.

"They know where you're going" came a voice to Jims left.

He jumped and came face to face with Costa. "Christ you scared me" Jim shouted.

"I'm sorry Jim "

"That's ok, what was that?".

"They know where you're going. You're going to the monastery" Costa replies.

"What else are they saying?"

"Nothing else".

One of the old men whistled. Jim turned back, but they had disappeared.

On the walk with Costa, Jim explained what had happened with the dream and the old man at the bar.

Costa did not know what to make of it, but hopefully, they would be able to work it out.

"Maybe you are being warned not to look there"

"It can't be that bad" Jim replied.

"Jim, enough people have warned you of what happened in the hills. Maybe they are worried for you" Costa pleaded.

"This isn't going to stop me from going Costa"

"Ok, I will come to the monastery, but no further" Costa demanded.

Within minutes, they were standing at the entrance, looking through the gates and up towards the main building at the top of the hill.

"Good job we are here now and not later, this place is creepy during the day" Jim remarked.

Costa sniggered, "I've never liked this place, it gives me the creeps at any time of day" and he pushed the gate.

As it moved, it gave out a high-pitched squeak, rust fell to the ground and the gate gained momentum, until the gate was fully open.

"no one has used this entrance in a while" Jim laughed.

They walked through the gate and stopped, so Jim could withdraw his phone out of his pocket to take a couple of photos for his research.

He held his phone up, took two photos and then brought the phone down to take a look at what he had taken.

Quickly, Jim thrust the phone at Costa.

"What is that to the right of the building?"

Costa took hold of the phone and squinted slightly. The sun was reflecting the sun into his face, so he had to tilt it just enough to make out the picture.

"what the" he replied.

He held the phone closer, pinched his fingers on the screen to enlarge the picture. He looked up, stared at the monastery, looked back at the phone, then back at the monastery again. There was some one standing next to the building.

"Jim "Costa holds out the phone and passes the phone back.

Jim stares at the building and the picture a few more times and then turns to face Costa.

"Glad you see him too, but he isn't there" and he points to the corner of the building where the figure was standing.

Worry was no longer the issue. Fear was now slowly setting in.

He was getting scared and was no longer enjoying the situation.

Jim walked over to olive tree and Costa quickly followed.

They sat down and Jim began to scan the pictures. The second photo Jim took, was an enlarged picture of the right-hand side of the monastery. Leaning against the wall, was the figure of a man wearing a uniform.

Jim enlarged the picture further to reveal and English army officer.

He looked what appeared to be a world war two captain in his mid-forties.

His epaulettes and peak cap could be clearly seen.

Costa kept looking over his shoulder. Every now and then he would look up at the corner of the building, as if to catch the man still standing there.

"he's definitely there isn't he?" and Jim pointed the phone at him.

Costa looked down at the phone. "Yes, he's there. But who is he?".

Jim put down his phone. "I will have to check later when I'm back at the hotel. The internet is quicker there".

They both stood up and began to slowly walk up the hill to the top.

After what felt like ages, they reached the front of the monastery.

They paused to catch their breath. Minutes passed and all that could be heard, was a few sparrows chirping in the nearby trees and their own laboured breath.

Jim looked down at his watch. "We need to make a move; it's getting late in the afternoon".

They hadn't realised how long they had been out there.

Somehow, the had not noticed time slipping by. Neither had they realised that the birds had stopped chattering.

As they walked to the edge of the building, Costa froze.

Jim didn't notice and bumped into the back of him.

"What's up?" Jim shouted.

"Listen".

Both of them had now stopped walking and were standing completely still.

Now they had noticed the birds had stopped singing.

Replacing that, was a faint whistle.

Costa now became very unnerved at hearing it.

"I don't like this Jim. This isn't right. My grandmother warned us. I think we should go back".

Costa had now completely lost his nerve and turned to walk back to the main road. Jim clasped his hands around Costas shoulder.

"calm my friend, it's just a noise" Jim had experience with calming people.

He was used to calming stressed students. He had plenty come to his office, especially at exam time. They would over revise, get themselves worked up and he would be their port of call.

"Keep calm, we will be fine "he said.

"I will stay a little longer, but as soon as the sun starts to set, we go".

"ok, we will". Jim held up his phone and started up his recorder.

"If that whistle starts again, we will get it on here" and he held the phone high up into the air.

They reached the corner where the captain was standing in the photo and suddenly the whistle came again. Only this time it was clearer and louder than before.

"The same whistle that the old guys did earlier" Jim stated.

"Yes, it is, but they couldn't have got up here before us, surely not" Costa replied.

"no, they couldn't have".

Jim stopped the recording and started to play it back. Clear as a bell, they could hear the whistle. Every time it was replayed, it seemed to alter slightly, but the tune was the same.

"You won't find anything here".

Jim and Costa jumped again and came face to face with a priest. He was dressed in tradition Greek orthodox costume, the tall black hat being the giveaway.

Jim almost swore at him and chose at the last second to bite his tongue. Costa didn't and said something in Greek. Jim knew that whatever he said, couldn't have been good as the priest gave Costa a stern look.

Jim was quick to apologise, he wasn't sure what he was apologising for, but felt he had too.

"It's ok" the priest replied.

"I saw you coming up the hill. I'm Father Aeolus "and he held out his hand.

Jim shook it "pleased to meet you" he replied.

Father Aeolus Raised his hand, beckoning them inside.

"Please, come inside" and he walked towards the open door.

Jim and Costa followed quickly as if to find solace inside.

They walked through the large door and into a large open space.

On the walls were intricate carvings and paintings, all laced with gold.

"That explains the outside" said Jim quietly.

"Who would want to rob a run-down shack?" and costa let out a little smirk which went unnoticed.

They walked down the centre isle to a larger open area, dominated by an effigy of Jesus Christ on the cross, which also was covered in gold.

They were both ushered into a side room. In the middle of the room, was a small table, with a jug of water and a couple of glasses.

"Please sit "

"ok" Costa replied and promptly flumped down into the chair.

Jim gently sat down and placed his hands onto the table.

Father Aeolus opened a cupboard and started routing through some boxes.

"Help yourselves to water" He said.

They both poured themselves a glass each and waited.

After a couple of minutes, a small box was placed in front of them.

"I think this is the reason why you are here" and Father Aeolus takes a handful of papers out of the box and places them onto the table.

Jim picked up a few of the papers. Put some to one side and returned to the box for some more.

He removed a couple and then froze.

"What have you found Jim?" Costa asks.

Jim slides a picture across the table to Costa. He picks it up and also freezes.

Father Aeolus appears behind him. "That was the resistance here in Anogia".

"and who is this?" pointing a finger to the centre of the picture.

Father Aeolus takes the picture and walks around the table. "That was my dear friend Captain Strachan. He was assigned to the group to help with the war".

"where is he now?" Costa asked.

There was a loud sigh.

"He went missing with the rest of them when the Germans arrived in the town. I was the liaison between him and the resistance when he arrived. We became exceptionally good friends".

Costa faced Jim. "That's definitely him in your picture".

Jim unlocks his phone and accesses the pictures.

Picks the one of the front of the monastery, enlarges it.

"Is this him?" and hands the phone over to Father Aeolus.

"This is he. When was this taken?".

"About half an hour ago, outside" Jim replied.

They placed the photos, side by side. The army officer in both pictures were identical. A well-built man, in his mid-forties, with a well-trimmed orange and silver beard. His uniform spotless, like it had only just been pressed.

The Father sat down at the table and picked up a couple of the papers.

"They want to forget them". He says.

"Who wants to forget?".

"The whole town, the town wants to let them rest, but they can't. That's why I have the records. The town wanted to throw them away, but I have saved them".

"Why can't they rest?" Costa pleaded.

"The only people that knew roughly where they went into the caves, was the Germans. They blew up every entrance they came across until it looked like nothing was ever there. All the men were still inside, including my friend".

"what about the whistling?" Jim asks.

"we have heard it a few times today but cannot place where it's coming from".

"Did it sound like this?" The Father pursed his lips and started to whistle.

The very sound sent shivers down Jim and Costas spines.

"Yes, that's it, that's the tune" Costa replied.

Father Aeolus got up and walked towards a beautiful stain glassed window and stared out.

"That's the signal we would give if there was trouble coming. The whole town would relay that message as soon as the Germans were spotted".

"So why are we hearing it now?".

"You are not the only ones that hear it, I myself hear it all the time".

"Why don't you look to where it's coming from?"

"I am fearful of what I might find!".

Jim and Costa looked at each other. "Can Costa and I have a moment please?".

"Of course," and Father Aeolus walks out of the room.

"What are you thinking Jim?".

"I'm thinking that we should look for the entrance".

Costa was becoming frustrated. He didn't mind helping Jim with research, but he certainly wasn't interested in a ghost hunt.

"I'm not sure Jim. I don't like idea of what could be down there if we find the entrance".

Jim giggled.

"We will be fine".

They both got up and walked through to the main part of the monastery. Father Aeolus was sitting in the front row of pews.

"Do you mind if we come back tomorrow Father?".

"Of course,"

"we will be here for about ten in the morning, if that is ok with you?"

"Not a problem" Father Aeolus replied.

With that, Jim and Costa walked out of the monastery and headed back towards the hotel on the route they walked before.

They had no idea that Father Aeolus and one other were watching them from the top of the hill.

He had a smile on his face. "They will find you my friend", and he turned and went back inside the building.

"I'm sure they will" came the reply.

CHAPTER 3

As they walked along. Neither Jim nor Costa looked back at the monastery.

Costa's nerves were shot, so he didn't care to look back.

Jim on the other hand was fascinated by what he could see, or in this case, what he couldn't.

The run-down house, they had seen earlier, with the two old men on the porch, had vanished. Nothing remained of what they passed.

As they drew closer, Jim purposely walked over to the side of the road that the house stood, so he could get a closer look.

All that remained of the property was the outer fence that ran along the boundaries.

Costa crossed the road and joined Jim. He too now was trying to get his head round what was going on.

Jim and Costa faced each other. "What the hell happened to the house?" Jim asks.

Costa is lost for words and simply shrugs his shoulders, then shakes his head in disbelief.

"There aren't even any foundation stones here, it's like the house never existed".

Finally, Costa found his voice.

"This is messed up; I can't even remember whether there has ever been a house here. I will have to check with my Grandmother".

Costa pulls his phone out of his pocket and dials a number.

Someone answers and Costa turns away from Jim and begins to talk. Jim decides to open the old gate and walk onto the grounds.

He felt a wave of sadness sweep through him. He wanted to break down in tears. He started to walk around the area. There wasn't any sign of there ever being a house there, not even a single nail.

Jim closed his eyes and took a deep breath. In his mind, he could see the house clearly. The two laughing men sitting on the porch.

Something didn't seem right with the image he was seeing.

The house looked the same as most of the others in the area, but it was the two men that didn't look right.

After a few minutes, it dawned on him. He opened his eyes and left.

Back on the street, Costa had finished talking on the phone and was waiting for Jim.

"Jim, there was a house here!".

"There was?".

"yes. I spoke with my mother and Grandmother. My Grandmother says that this was where the leader of the resistance lived. When the Germans arrived and the resistance fled into the hills, they knew who he was and where he lived, and His house was the first to be searched and then destroyed".

Jim suddenly realised who the two men were and the reason why they didn't look quite right. It was the leader of the resistance. They were wearing clothes of the time.

"You don't reckon, that was who we saw?"

"It must have been. Jim I'm not sure I like this".

"Its ok, we will be fine" Jim replied.

Costa started to shake his head "Jim, I'm not tempting fate, I am taking heed of the warnings. I have helped enough, if you are going back tomorrow, I will pick you up and take you there, but that will be it".

"I won't push you into anything Costa". Jim replied.

"Ok, I will see you at nine thirty"

"ok see you then".

Costa turned away and headed off down the road.

Jim withdrew his notebook and pen from his pocket and scribbled some extra notes, Mainly about the house and the two old men.

Soon, he was back at his hotel room.

He placed his rucksack down by the side of the dressing table and walked over to the small drink's fridge.

He opened the door, withdrew a bottle of water and walked out onto his balcony.

He slid out the chair from under the table and sat down.

The sun was starting to set. While he watched the world go by around him, he pondered on the day's events. It wasn't long before his eyes closed and fell asleep.

He didn't sleep long, before the local nightlife rose him from his slumber.

Mopeds roaring past and rowdy youngsters, letting their hair down and getting drunk were responsible.

Jim lifted his arm and looked at his watch. It was eleven o'clock and now he was wide awake.

He left the outside world to their fun and walked back into his room and slid the balcony door shut.

The outside world suddenly ceased to exist and Not a sound could be heard.

He placed his water on the side table by his bed, took his notebook from his jacket and laid down on the bed.

He began to scan through the notes again. He was still confused by everything he had witnessed. He was comforted by the fact, that he was returning to the monastery in the morning and he began to write what questions he could further ask Father Aeolus.

He didn't get very far. Jim had managed to write two questions into the book before he fell back to sleep.

The night was warm, but comfortable and Jim had a complete night's sleep, undisturbed by the dramas of the previous day. Even the dream he had the night before, never returned to haunt him, although it still played on his mind.

The following morning, he woke feeling refreshed and energetic.

He rubbed his eyes and stretched. He felt slightly embarrassed with himself for going to bed still fully clothed.

He walked into the bathroom, undressing as he went. After a quick wash down, he was ready for the day ahead. He walked back into the bedroom and froze.

There on the bed was his notebook. Pages open and facing the ceiling.

He Could make out the notes that he had made, but underneath was something else. Large scribbles of various sizes were drawn across both pages.

He slowly walked over and took hold of the book and held it up.

There written across the bottom half of the page were the words

Eimaste edo.

The letters were roughly written with a shaking hand. Jim could clearly see what was written but couldn't understand what it meant.

He would ask Nikos when he got down to the restaurant. He had a few questions to ask, as he wasn't very impressed with him telling everyone in the hotel his business, but mainly wanted to ask about the old man that followed him.

He put the notebook down on the dressing table and continued to get dressed. He put on his shoes and was ready to go downstairs. Picked up his notebook and put it in his jacket pocket, he decided not to take his rucksack today as he didn't want to be burdened with extra if he was going to be walking around the hills.

He picked up his bottle of water and made his way down to the restaurant.

As he walked through the restaurant doors Nikos was waiting for him. "good morning sir would you like your usual table?"

"Yes, and I need to have a word with you".

Nikos looked concerned "have I done something wrong sir".

"Not as such" jim replied as they approached the table.

"Can I have breakfast first and I will talk to you after".

"no problem sir I will get it now" and he disappeared into the kitchen.

Minutes passed and he returned with Jims food and placed it down in front of him. Jim was famished and tucked in.

It wasn't long before his food was finished, and he beckoned Nikos over. Cautiously Nikos walked over to jim.

"is there a problem sir" he asked.

"its not a problem, just more of a query or two".

Nikos pulls out a chair at the table and sits beside him. Jim sits with his coffee In his hands.

"did you talk to anybody in the kitchen about why I am here?" jim asked.

"I mentioned it only to the chef, his family owns the hotel, can I ask why?".

"I was followed by an old man who claimed he worked here. He talked to me about what happened here during the war".

Nikos looked confused "there is only the chef and me that work here in the restaurant".

"And nobody else" Jim asked.

"Well There is the groundsman, but he only comes in after lunch. Can you tell me what he looked like?".

Jim tried to picture what the old man looked like. "yes, he was fairly small and walked with a limp. He was slightly hunched over and had white hair with a bald top and He wore thin metal rimmed glasses ".

Costa looked shocked. "can you come with me sir" he pleaded.

They rose up from behind the table and walked out towards the reception. Scattered about in various places along the walls, were various pictures of the hotel. A few were of past employees.

Nikos guided jim down one side of the main entrance and stopped halfway down. "is this him?" and pointed to the picture on the wall.

Jims jaw dropped, in the photo, stood five people. In the centre was the old man that followed him to the taverna. In the bottom right hand corner in white letters, it read 'Ioulios 1940'. Jim could only assume that the picture was taken in 1940.

"yes, that is him, but how can that be, I was talking to him yesterday".

"strange things have happened in this hotel and some of the guests have said that this man was responsible. We know it can't be true as he died a year after this photo was taken. He was the owner at the time and the hotel has remained in the family since" Nikos replied.

This confirmed with Jim that he had been talking to a ghost. That and what the barman at the taverna had told him yesterday was all the proof that he needed.

A horn sounded outside and jim looked out of the doors to see Costa sitting in his car.

"Thank you for the information I must go" and he darted out of the doors.

He quickly ran over to Costa's car, opened the door and sat down.

"you are not going to believe this" Jim said.

"I have just been talking to the waiter inside about me talking to the old man yesterday and it turns out, the man has been dead for the last seventy-nine years".

Costa looked shocked "I told you that this was not a good idea".

Jim being a sceptical man and although shocked by the experience wasn't wavered in any way.

"I will be okay, just drop me off at the monastery".

"I worry about your safety" Costa pleaded.

"I will be fine".

The cars engine came to life and Costa pulled away from the hotel.

Jim was glad that he was not walking. The sun was beating down already, and the heat was already becoming uncomfortable. Within moments they had arrived at the monastery gates.

Costa turned to Jim, "have you got your mobile phone?".

Jim takes his phone out of his pocket and waves it in front of Costa.

"of course, I won't go anywhere without my trusty travelling companion" and they both laughed.

"if you get into trouble, ring me" Costa pleaded.

Jim understood Costa's caution, but still wished that he would join him. "I will" and Jim got out of the car and walked towards the gates. He stopped and turned to watch the car drive away.

He looked at his watch and realised he was a little early, but that would give him plenty of time to walk around the monastery.

His walk up the hillside was more of a struggle, compared to the day before and should have been easier as he hadn't got his rucksack. Halfway up, he paused, took his phone and proceeded to take photos. Jim had the idea that maybe the spirit of captain Strachan would return.

He took six photos, looked at each one, but the captain never appeared.

He started walking again. As he did, he noticed Father Aeolus standing in the doorway of the monastery waiting for him.

At Jims approach, the father held out his hand. Jim shook it and they both walked inside.

They both walked down to the room they were in previously.

Scattered on the table, were various maps and pictures.

"I have searched through all of the records for you" and Father Aeolus pointed to the table.

"I have marked the main map as to where the main entrance to the caves is situated" he placed his finger onto the map. "There is another smaller entrance about half a mile to the west, but it was a lot smaller and would be too much work for you alone to clear".

Jim sat down at the table and poured himself some water.

He couldn't understand why no one had tried to uncover the caves once the Germans had left. So, he was going to be brave and ask the father.

"why didn't anyone go back and help them?". Jim asked.

Father Aeolus looked sorrowful.

"please remember, we are god fearing, traditional people. They feel that they should be left at peace".

Jim was a little annoyed at hearing that. "couldn't you do anything? You knew where they were".

"the church wouldn't allow me to do anything, apart from safeguarding the records and making sure no one came in search of them, but I am getting old and I now disagree with the church".

"what about the house down the road? I saw it on the way up here yesterday and on the way back to the hotel, it had vanished. I was told that it belonged to the resistance leader and that the Germans destroyed it. But now there is no evidence that the house was ever there".

Father Aeolus clasped his hands together. "after the Germans left and the people returned to the town, the mayor ordered the clean up to begin. The house was completely removed".

Jim could understand that they wanted to create a new Anogia and the evidence of what had happened needed to be removed, but what he could not understand was why would they try to forget the people that had died.

"But why forget what happened?" Jim asked.

"the people wanted to move forward with their lives, so they rebuilt the town and placed the memorial here".

Jim was now seeing Father Aeolus's point and was now able to understand the situation that they were in.

"Thank you, Father for the information, I better get moving, I have a lot to do".

With that, Jim rose from his chair, folded the map and made his way to the door. As he approaches the entrance of the monastery, he noticed the memorial to the resistance. It was a statue of a man wearing a sheep skin waist coat with his right leg raised onto a rock and the Greek orthodox cross behind him.

Jim stopped in front of it, joined his hands and bowed his head.

He promised George that he would pay his respects and that was a promise he has now kept.

As Jim was walking through the door, Father Aeolus called out "this may help". Jim raised his head to see him walking in the centre aisle with a shovel in his hand. He takes the shovel and turns back to face the memorial. Something catches his eye at the base of the statue. In golden letters were the words 'Eimaste edo'.

Jim pulled out the notebook and opened and opened it to the centre pages to reveal the scribbles that had been written during the night. He turns to Father Aeolus and points at the statue "what does this mean?".

The Father looks and replies "it means 'we are here'". Jim shows him the notebook pages. "this was written in my notebook whilst I was asleep last night, I don't remember writing it myself and I do not understand the Greek language".

"maybe they have chosen you to communicate with" and with that Father Aeolus turned and walked back down to the far end of the monastery.

Jim walked outside to a blast of hot air.

The first thing Jim noticed apart from the heat, was the lack of bird song. On his way up to the monastery, he could hear the birds and all the local traffic. Now, there was nothing. He could feel a warm breeze rushing past but couldn't hear it brushing his ears.

He opened the map, turned to the left and proceeded to walk to the edge of the building to where they saw the Captain.

He stopped to gain his bearings and looked out across the hills, comparing them to the map. Strolling his finger across and gaging the distance between him and the cross, Father Aeolus placed on it.

It was only a ten-minute walk, but in that heat, it may as well of been an hour. He knew it would be a struggle, but he was happy to be committing himself to doing it.

Father Aeolus appeared behind him. "here, take this" and he passed Jim a canteen of water. "you will need this in this heat".

Jim accepted "thank you "and he began to walk away.

Following the map reminded Jim of when he was in the scouts. They were given two hours to orienteer their way across the Purbeck hills. They were dropped off at Corfe Castle and by using set points on the map, they would end up in the centre of Swanage.

The task was completed, and they had plenty of fun on route.

Holding the map now brought back his skills at map reading and started to follow an old path along the edge of the hill.

The hills themselves were baren, apart from a few clumps of dry grass here and there. Piles of rocks were strewn across the landscape.

In front of him, he could make out a large outcrop of rocks. He stopped again and looked down at the map. It was where the entrance used to be.

The path narrowed and got closer to the edge of the hill.

The sides grew steeper until there was just a vertical drop.

A large rock jutted off the edge of the path into nothingness.

'I reckon this must be where the man was thrown off" Jim thought.

As he looked along the edge, he could see that that was possibly the only point near the outcrop that could have been where the Soldier pushed the man to his death.

He felt overwhelming sadness and stepped away from the edge.

He valued his life and didn't want to put himself in danger. That thought amused him slightly and he giggled to himself. 'I'm stepping away from the edge to keep myself safe and there is me going to dig out a cave entrance'.

He opened the canteen and took a mouthful of water.

It was surprisingly cool and refreshing. He sat down on a small rock and withdrew a hanky from his pocket. wiped the sweat now forming on his face, took another swig of water and closed the cap of the canteen.

As he stood back up, he heard a faint whistle.

He turned and looked in the direction the sound had come from.

It was coming from the outcrop. It was the same tune as before.

He shook his head, as to get rid of the sound from his mind. He opened the canteen again, took another swig of water and replaced the cap.

Jim began walking again and after a few steps he was standing in front of what he thought was a mountain of rocks.

Jim looked around the base. He could see where bullets had left their wounding marks. 'this is it' he thought.

He knelt down in front of the largest rock and began to sweep away the dirt. He had only removed a few inches of soil when a gap appeared. Some of the soil began to drop into the gap, making Jim scoop a little faster to stop it being filled in.

The whistle sounded again. Only this time, it was louder and clearer. Jim paused. The tune repeated a couple of times, allowing Jim to confirm as to where it was coming from "it's definitely from in here" he said to himself.

He grabbed the shovel and placed it onto the floor. Stomped his foot hard onto the head and with ease, it struck into the ground.

The whistle came again.

Jim ignored it, he knew if he was going to do this, he had to continue. He shrugged his shoulders, swung the soil away and struck the ground a second time.

Soon, Jim had revealed the top of the entrance. More battle scars on the rocks were revealed, including what appeared to be blast marks from explosives. The Father was right. The entrance was there. It bore all the scars of battle. He paused for a moment, then began to etch a line, from left to right. Marking the entrance.

It was roughly nine feet across. He wasn't sure how deep it went, but Jim was hoping it wasn't too far down. He didn't know if he had the energy to dig for that long.

After a couple of hours of digging, Jim stopped, threw the shovel down onto the ground and took a step back.

He had cleared enough of the entrance for someone to crouch down and crawl into the void he had created.

He was Getting tired. The work and the heat had started to take its toll.

"You look shattered Jim" came a voice from behind him.

Jim jumped and turned around to see Costa walking towards him.

"Christ you scared me"

Costa found it amusing and Jim could see a huge smile on his face.

"I thought you said, you weren't going to help" Jim asked.

Costa walked up to Jim and placed a hand on his shoulder "I got home and sat in the garden. I was thinking about what I had said to you and realised I could not leave my friend to do this on his own. So, I came to help".

"Costa, you are a true friend" Jim replied and placed his hand on Costa's shoulder.

Costa picked up the shovel. "Have You heard the whistles this time Jim?"

Jim faced the cave entrance "Yes, a couple of times. A lot louder and clearer this time. I've tried to ignore it, but it keeps playing on my mind".

"Do you think they are still down there?".

"I have no doubt, they couldn't have been able to escape".

Costa started to scrape away at the loose dirt and Jim scooped away with his hands.

Now the gap was large enough for the both of them to crawl into.

Costa reached into his pocket and pulled out a small torch.

He clicked the button on the base and a beam of blue white light arched into the darkness.

Simultaneously, as the light entered the cave, the whistle returned again. Jim staggered back.

"oh my god, that was here, right next to me" Jim shouted.

He looked at Costa. Costa stood motionless.

"Costa snap out of it" and he grabbed costa and gave him a shake.

"I'm sorry Jim, that was scary. I haven't heard it that loud before, it must be coming from inside the caves".

"It's ok, but we need to keep our wits about us" Jim replied.

Costa knelt down inside the entrance and waved the torch from side to side.

Shadows danced off the walls as the light swept through.

"look there!" Costa yelled.

Jim crouched beside Costa and peered into the void.

Laying on the floor, barely feet away from them, laid a rifle and a knapsack. Dust had settled on them, but the colouring could still be made out under the thick layer.

"wow, we must go in. anything we find must be collected and brought back outside".

"Then what do we do with it?" Costa replied.

"We give everything to Father Aeolus; he will know what to do with it all".

Jim slowly crawled through the entrance, followed by Costa.

Neither of them had noticed, that the birds had started singing again. But they seemed to be singing in unison. No other sounds could be heard apart from them. Neither did they notice, the skeletal remains of an arm, reaching out from underneath a pile of rubble. It was outreached as if in a desperate bid for life. Reaching out into the darkness before he was taken by the darkness itself.

They scrambled down the rubble onto the cave floor.

Costa walked over to the rifle and shone the torch onto it. "come look at this Jim" He yelled.

Jim ran over and stood beside him. Costa was dusting the rifle down. Next to it, scratched into the cave floor was an arrow, pointing to the entrance.

Costa picked up the rifle and stood up straight next to Jim.

"what does it mean?".

"it's pointing to the outside".

Costa points the torch at the arrow and follows the direction its pointing.

Jim takes a Deep breath as the light hits the base of the arm poking out from the rubble.

"The others must have marked it, so if anyone comes to search for them, he will be found".

They both scrambled over and started to remove the rocks and dirt from around the body.

Slowly, more and more of the body was revealed.

A skeleton, totally devoid of flesh appeared from the ground. The clothing still in good condition wrapped the remnants.

"He's one of the resistance fighters".

Jim bowed his head in respect. "we must take him outside, ready to be taken back to the monastery".

"that's all fine, but we can't take everything back today".

"we won't have too. We can remove him for now and continue the search. The rest can be done at a later date".

Jim crouched down and started to open the knapsack.

"What are you hoping to find in there Jim".

"Hopefully, something that will tell us, who he was" Jim replied.

He pulled the cord, opened the bag and started to search inside.

He pulls out a canvas poncho and hands it to Costa.

"We can wrap the body in this and take him out"

Costa Gulped. He wasn't squeamish but was uneasy about moving bodies.

"let's go" Costa replied.

They unfolded the poncho and laid it down beside the body.

Carefully they placed it inside and wrapped it up.

It was lighter than Jim thought, they picked it up and slowly walked back to the entrance, placed the body outside on the floor and stood motionless for a few minutes.

Costa mumbled something in Greek and raised his head.

"Let's get back inside there, we have to look further".

As they returned inside the cave, they were unaware of the black figure walking towards them.

Father Aeolus had been sitting in his office, thinking about his friends and the search that had begun to find them.

As he sat at the table, looking through the photos, he was unaware of a dark shadow forming behind him in the corner.

"They have found us" came a voice from the shadowy figure.

Father Aeolus wasn't phased at all. As if he knew that it was there.

"Yes, I gave the Englishman a map. He is there now" He replied.

The shadow had now taken form, it was Captain Strachan.

He walked around the table and stood in front of Father Aeolus.

"Will you go and give a blessing?".

Father Aeolus put down the photos and looked directly into the Captains eyes.

"I will go now". He rose from the table and turned to face the door.

"Thank you, my friend," the Captain replied as his image faded and disappeared.

Father Aeolus walked through the monastery to the alter. He retrieved his bible and beads and made his way outside.

As he got closer to the caves, he could see Costa and Jim standing outside. They were motionless. After a few minutes, they walked back inside and disappeared.

As he approached the entrance, he could see the corpse laying on the floor.

He knelt down in front of the body and proceeded with blessing the remains.

Jim and Costa were unaware of the Fathers arrival and continued to walk deeper into the caves.

The torch light swept through the caves illuminating every part. Shadows continued to dance. At times, they looked like people running back and forth as if hiding from them.

They stopped when the light hit a branch in the cave. Three different tunnels led away from their position.

"Which one do we take?" Costa whispers.

Jim shrugged his shoulders. "any of them. We can't split up. We have to stay together, or they will be sending in a search party for us".

Costa lowered the torch to the ground; it illuminated another arrow. Rather than being etched into the ground, this one had been formed out of a shirt and pointed to a large tunnel to the right of where they were standing.

"This way Jim".

"are you sure?" Jim asked and Costa pointed to the arrow on the floor.

Jim was impressed. "They had left markers to their position in case people came to look for them" he said and they both turned into the tunnel and started to walk cautiously.

Suddenly an icy cold wind blew through the tunnel from in front of them. It blasted straight past them, almost knocking them off their feet. Costa and Jim grabbed hold of each other, to stop from going over.

Quickly, the chilled air was replaced by a hot breeze. It was warming, comforting and made them both feel calm and at ease. As the wind was blowing through the tunnels, they could clearly hear the whistle again.

Soon they approached what appeared to be a dead end. The tunnel abruptly stopped.

Costa shone the torch around the walls, looking for another arrow or tunnel.

He looked at Jim "that wind had to of come from somewhere" and he scanned the walls over again.

The walls glistened in the torchlight. Beads of water cascading down to the floor.

Jim noticed something that didn't look right where the tunnel stopped. He moved closer to the wall and stroked the surface. When he looked at his hand, it was covered in mud.

"over here" he called to costa.

Costa ran over. "what is it?" he replied.

"I think we have to get through here. They hid themselves behind this wall. I reckon the man we found at the entrance stayed this side to help cover their exit, only they didn't expect the Germans to block off the other end".

"sounds about right, we need to take this wall down" and they started scraping at the wall.

After a few minutes, the shovel was scraping against wood. This made them move faster with a sense of urgency.

They managed to clear a section large enough for both of them to walk through with ease.

The wood and mud had been piled to one side to keep the rest of the tunnel clear.

Costa and Jim peered through. The tunnel opened up into a large cavern. Stalactites and stalagmites decorated the huge expanse of the cave. Jims eyes had to focus slightly, he was certain that he could see a building in the centre. He took the torch off Costa and shone it into the centre. The light bounced off wall panels and tiles of a roof.

"my god, they must be in there!" and they walked in.

As they approached the building, they began to get an idea of the size of it. They stopped a few feet away from the front door. Jim recognised the building.

"I don't want to sound stupid here but isn't that the building we saw on the main road" Jim asked.

Costa looked. The porch looked familiar to him. "Yes Jim, this is the same one, but how did it get from there to here?"

"I'm not sure I want to know "Jim replied.

Suddenly Costa kicked something. It was a lantern. He picked it up, examined it and took a lighter out of his pocket.

With a click, the lighter burst into life and an orange glow rose into the darkness. Illuminating the immediate area. That and the torch now clearly revealed the front of the house.

The whistling suddenly stopped, and the warm breeze returned.

Jim slowly approached the front steps and walked to the door.

Costa quickly joined him and they both stood and looked at each other.

Jim reaches for the doorknob, "I think they are in here".

"I hope so" replied Costa, "all this is starting to get me freaked out".

Jim wrapped his hand around the doorknob and started to turn it.

To their surprise the door made a sound that they didn't expect. The door groaned as if a hundred people sighed with relief.

The lanterns glow lit up the interior. The sight that greeted them, made Costa run out into the cave, where he was violently sick.

Scattered about the inside of the house, were the bodies of the resistance fighters. Some sitting in chairs, others laying on beds and on the floor. All were in various states of decay. Some were full skeletons, others, still had the remnants of decaying flesh hanging off the bones, resisting the natural urge to liquify and drop to the floor.

Jim stopped himself from being sick and gained his composure.

He walked round the room, to the far end and stopped at a high-backed chair that was facing out of the window. Its occupant hidden from Jim's field of vision.

Jim held on to the side and slowly turned the chair around.

The first thing Jim saw was the orange beard and knew exactly who it was. It was Captain Strachan.

Jim looked towards the door and in the faint light, could see Costa tidying himself up after ejecting his breakfast.

"Costa, I have found the Captain, quickly, we need to get him to the monastery" Jim shouted.

Costa came running in. He grabbed a blanket off an empty bed and laid it onto the floor. They moved the chair over and gently tipped it, allowing the Captains body to fall into the blanket.

As they folded over the excess, Costa recited something in Greek, then said god bless.

They lifted the body and slowly made there way out of the house.

They proceeded to head for the entrance. Jim noticed a change. The whistling hadn't returned. The cold wind had gone, and things felt normal again.

As they approached the cave entrance, Jim and Costa, could see Father Aeolus standing to the side.

Jim called out "Father, we have found your friend".

Father Aeolus turned to face them and clasped his hands together.

Once outside in the open air, both jim and Costa breathed a sigh of relief.

Jim picked up the canteen of water and took a dozen sips, he then passed it over to Costa.

They didn't notice Father Aeolus kneeling by the body of his friend and praying.

Costa took Jims arm and walked him a few steps. "I think we need to go and get cleaned up. Explain to the Father that we will return to help in the morning".

Jim agreed and walked over to Father Aeolus.

He waited until he had finished his prayers and then took his chance to speak.

"Father, we need to go and get cleaned up. They are all in the same area in the caves, but we thought we would bring Captain Strachan's body out first".

Costa then joined them "do you want us to call the police and get a team up here?" he asked.

Father Aeolus raised his head, tears welling in his eyes "it is ok, I will deal with it from here, you have done me and my friends a great service, this will never be forgotten".

With that, Father Aeolus raised himself off the floor and shook both their hands.

"You go, I will see you soon" and he knelt back down next to the two bodies.

"if you are sure?" Costa asked.

"please go and thank you again ".

Costa looked at Jim. They both felt an overwhelming sadness come over them for the Father and for the men that lost their lives inside the caves.

They started to walk back to Jims hotel. As they walked, they kept turning their heads to look back at the top of the hill.

As they approached the edge of the town, they stopped and took one last look.

Both their eyes shot wide open.

Up on the top of the hill, were a large group of men. They were in old clothing and all had rifles in their arms.

Standing in the middle of the group, were Father Aeolus and Captain Strachan, side by side.

"we found them Jim" Costa commented.

"we reunited them "Jim replied.

THE END

Printed in Poland
by Amazon Fulfillment
Poland Sp. z o.o., Wrocław

62211082R00035